LEGS

The tale of a meerkat lost and found

Sarah J. Dodd

Illustrated by Giusi Capizzi

LION
CHILDREN'S

Miki and Mama lived under the ground,
where it was warm, dark, and safe.

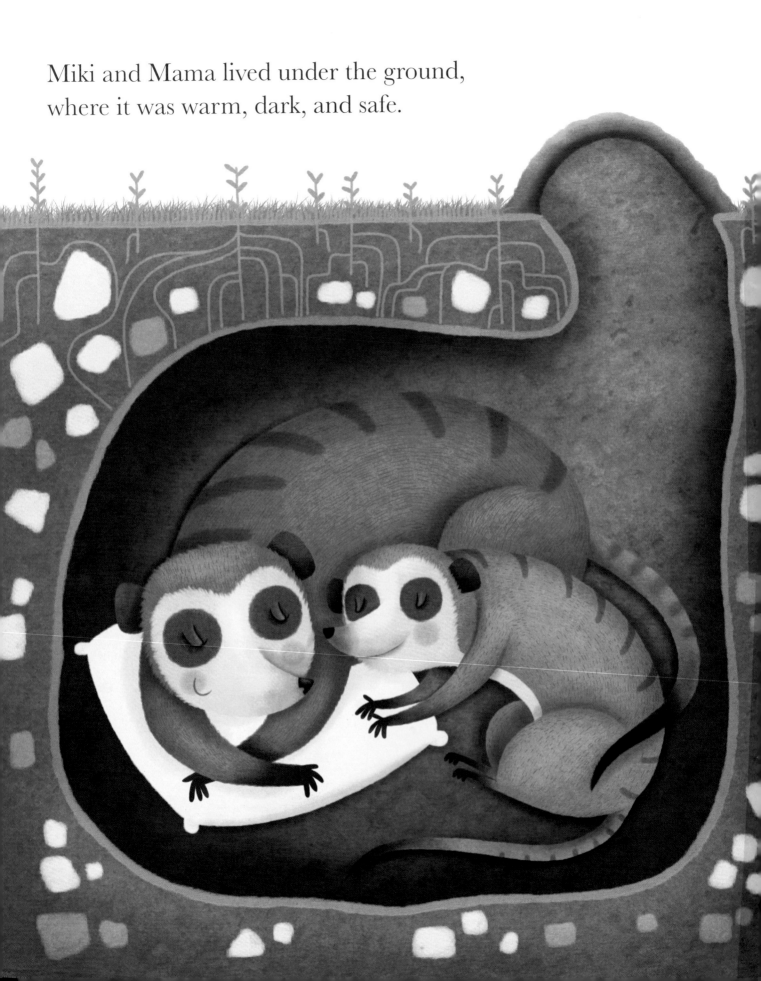

One day, Miki woke up and Mama was gone.
"Mama?" he said.
But Mama was nowhere to be seen.

"Miki!" called Mama. "Come outside and see the world."

"I don't like outside," said Miki. "I don't want to see the world."

"I'll be here," said Mama, "and the keeper will take care of us."

Outside, it was light;

it was bright;

it was exciting…

... and a little bit frightening.

But Mama was always there, and the keeper took care of them.

Miki wanted to see more of the world.

But the world was full of LEGS!

Pink legs...

and wrinkly legs...

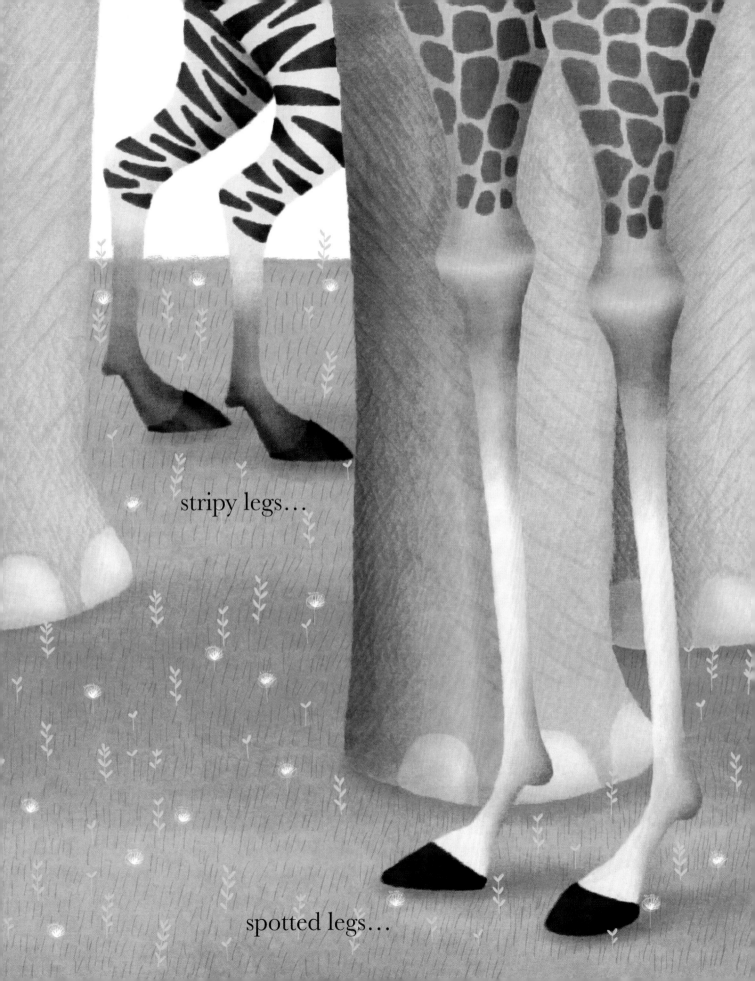

stripy legs…

spotted legs…

… and FIERCE, furry legs that made Miki run as fast as his own little legs would allow.

Outside the zoo, there were even more LEGS of all shapes and sizes…

Even the buildings looked like LEGS, reaching high into the distant sky.

They were *so* tall that Miki felt very, very small.

"MAMA?" said Miki.
But Mama was nowhere to be seen.

"Can I help you, my little friend?"
said a voice.

   Miki knew *those* legs!

But now there were hands as well –
warm and strong, lifting Miki up.

And there was a kind face.

There were faces *everywhere*!

Faces of all shapes and sizes...

FIERCE, furry faces…

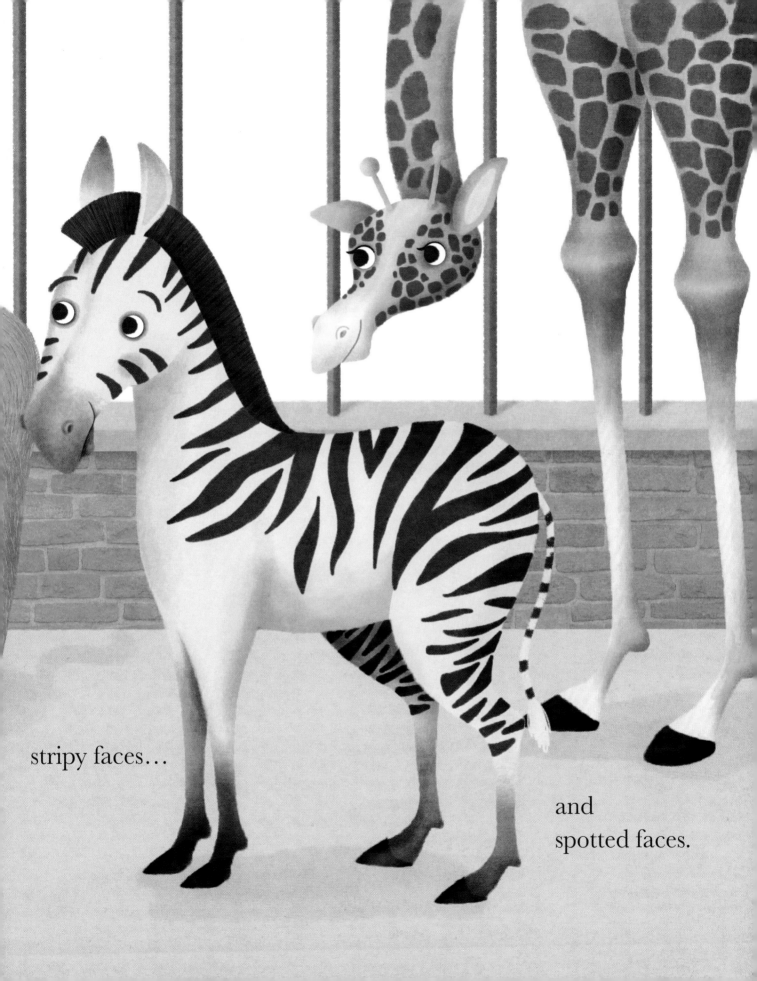

stripy faces…

and
spotted faces.

Wrinkly faces…

and pink faces.

And at last…

... the face Miki *loved* best of all.

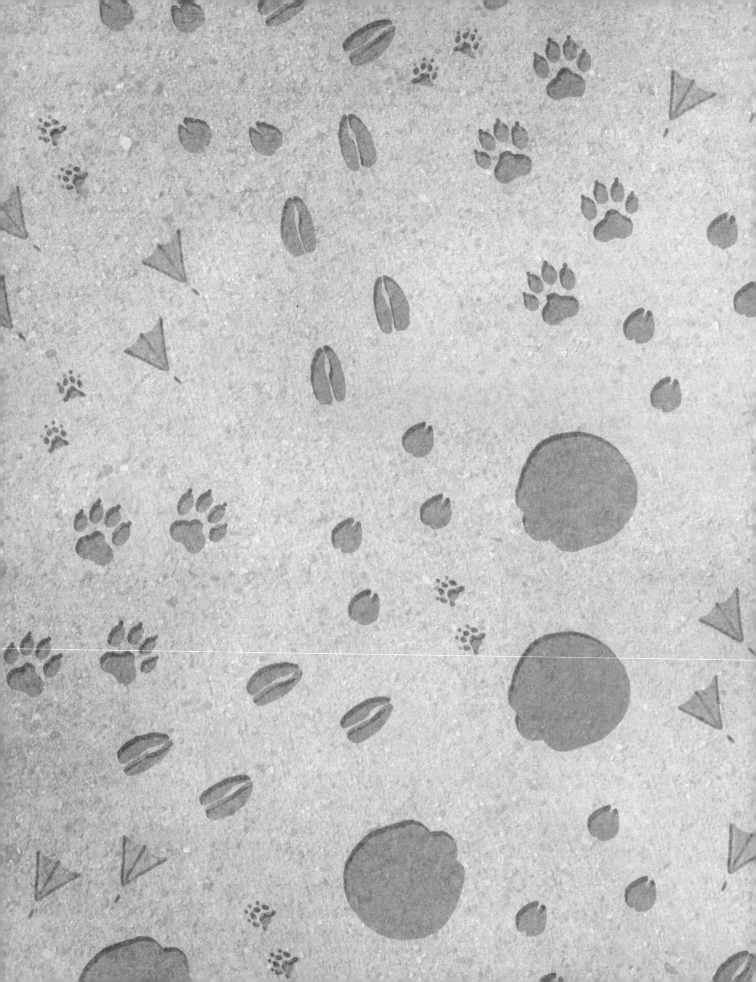